For KÆ - A.L.
For Grandma - L.B.

PICTURE CORGI

UK | USA | Canada | Ireland | Australia
India | New Zealand | South Africa

Picture Corgi is part of the Penguin Random House group of companies
whose addresses can be found at global.penguinrandomhouse.com.
www.penguin.co.uk   www.puffin.co.uk   www.ladybird.co.uk

Penguin Random House
UK

First published 2017
001

Text copyright © Abie Longstaff, 2017
Illustrations copyright © Lauren Beard, 2017
The moral right of the author and illustrator has been asserted

Printed in China

A CIP catalogue record for this book is available from the British Library

ISBN: 978-0-552-57519-5

All correspondence to:
Picture Corgi, Penguin Random House Children's,
80 Strand, London WC2R 0RL

Wonderful Work, Killie,
love Queenie
x

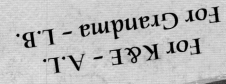

Thanks, K.
Prince Peter

To, Kilie,
@ Pen
x

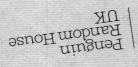

Thanks, Miss Lacey,
H Dumpty

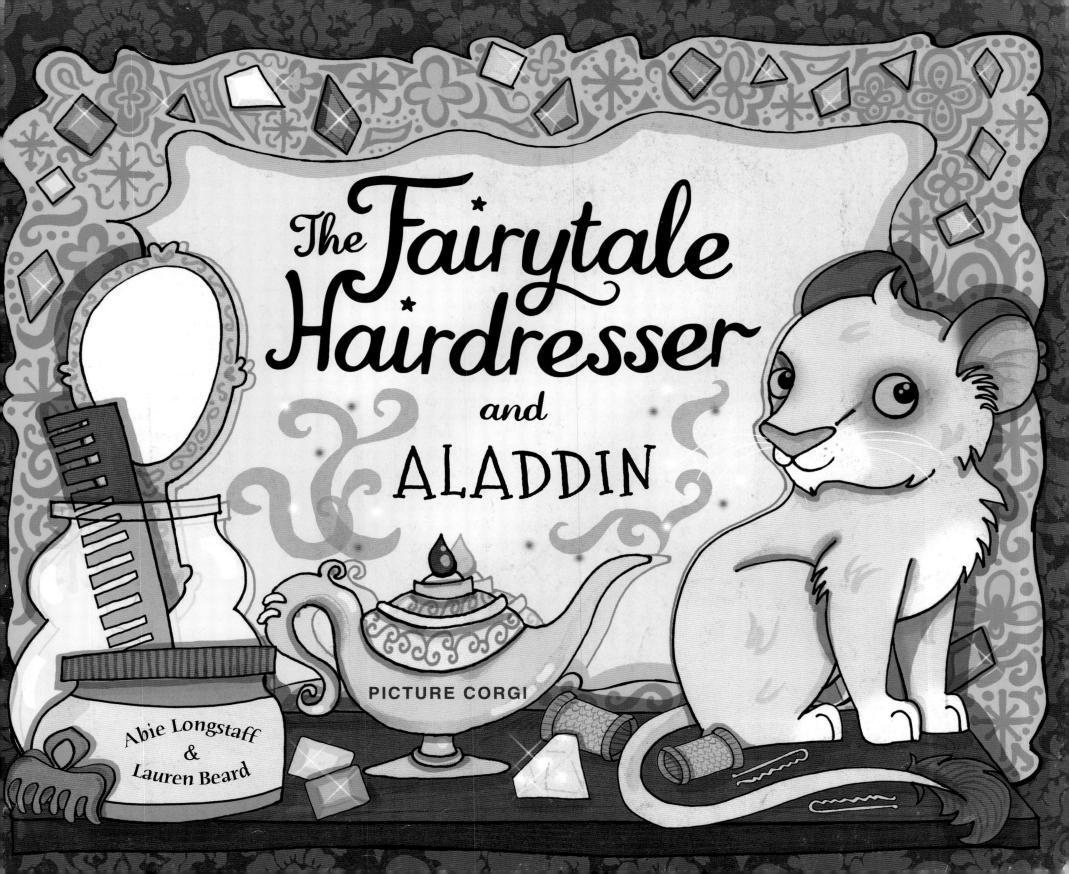

The Fairytale Hairdresser

and
ALADDIN

PICTURE CORGI

Abie Longstaff
&
Lauren Beard

Kittie Lacey was the best hairdresser in all the land.

She was always very busy! Every day her salon was filled with customers wanting the world's finest hairstyles.

Poor Kittie was exhausted! And she was running out of ideas for styles. She needed a holiday.

CLOSED FOR THE HOLIDAYS

ROUND-THE-WORLD TICKET

Luckily she had a ticket for Aladdin's Magic Carpet Tours, so she packed her bags, hung a sign on the salon door and set off . . .

Everyone was waiting to board the flying carpet.
"The tour is about to begin!" called Aladdin.

Kittie was very excited. She had her sketchbook ready so she
could draw new hair designs. She climbed into her seat – and off they flew!

They swooped down to Sherwood Forest . . .

The magic carpet zoomed high in the air and Kittie could see far and wide.

They whooshed up through the clouds . . .

They flew on and on until . . .
"Welcome to my home town!" cried Aladdin. "First stop – the bazaar!"

Kittie was admiring the beautiful scarves
and colourful ribbons when she heard
a voice calling from up high. It was
Aladdin's friend Princess Jamelia!

"I'm having a party tomorrow night," said Jamelia. "Please will you all come?"
"We'd love to!" said Aladdin and Kittie.

When Jamelia had gone, Aladdin turned to Kittie.
"Oh, Kittie," he sighed. "I want to get Jamelia a special present but I don't have enough money."

Kittie gave him a hug. "I'm sure Jamelia will like whatever you give her."
But Aladdin just shook his head sadly.

The next morning Aladdin wasn't at breakfast. And he wasn't at lunch.
Kittie was worried. "I'm going to look for him," she said.
"We'll look too," said Cinderella.

HOTEL

They looked here,

there

and everywhere.

Until suddenly Kittie
heard a voice coming from
a hole in the ground.

Help!

It was Aladdin. "Help!"
he shouted. "I'm trapped!"
From deep underground,
Aladdin told his story . . .

I met a man called Ibeneeza. He led me to a secret cave filled with treasure! He promised to share everything with me if I helped him.

He lowered me down into the cave . . . It was filled with gold and jewels!

I passed the treasure up to Ibeneeza. Then he told me to look for an enormous blue jewel. I found it, but as soon as I passed it up Ibeneeza gave a wicked laugh . . .

"This is a magic jewel," he said. "Whoever looks into it must obey me! Now I can make Princess Jamelia marry me. Then I will be a prince!"

Ibeneeza tricked me! He took the rope and left me stuck here!

"Oh, Kittie!" cried Aladdin. "Ibeneeza is going to trick Jamelia too! I have to get out of this cave and save her."

"Don't worry, love," said Kittie. "I'll get you out."

Quickly Kittie plaited some palm leaves into a rope. She lowered it down and Aladdin climbed up out of the hole!

Aladdin was free! But he was still miserable.

"All that was left in the cave was this dusty old lamp," he said sadly.

Kittie gave the lamp a polish – and something strange began to happen . . .

whoooooOOOOOOooosh!

A genie appeared!

"Thank you for releasing me," said the genie to the friends. "I hated being stuck in that lamp. As a reward I will grant you three wishes."
"Please take us to Jamelia!" said Aladdin.

KAZAM!

In a flash they were inside the palace.
But Ibeneeza was already there! He was showing Jamelia the magic jewel!
"Look at this!" he told her. "You love me. You want to marry me."

"Jamelia! Don't look!" called Aladdin as he rushed towards her.
"You're in great danger!"

 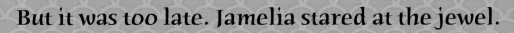

But it was too late. Jamelia stared at the jewel.

Kittie had to stop Ibeneeza! What could she do?

"Quick!" Kittie shouted to Aladdin. "Use the lamp!" He rubbed the lamp and the genie appeared . . .

The spell was broken and Jamelia woke up!

Kittie pulled a scarf from her bag and threw it to cover the jewel.

"Oh, thank you, Aladdin! Thank you, Kittie!" said Jamelia. "I definitely don't want to marry Ibeneeza."
She looked at Aladdin, and he gazed back into her eyes.

"Aladdin," said Jamelia, "will you marry me?"
"But I'm just a poor boy," said Aladdin.
"You have something much more important than money," she told him.
"You have a kind heart."
Jamelia kissed Aladdin and everyone cheered.

"You have one more wish to use," said the genie.
Aladdin looked at his friend Kittie.
"You helped me so much," he said.
"You should choose the third wish."

Kittie thought for a moment. She pictured her lovely salon and all her friends. "I already have everything I want," she said. "And I know someone who needs this wish more than I do . . . I wish the genie could be free!"

KAZ AM!

And she was.

The next day Kittie had the chance to try out all her new ideas for hairstyles . . .

. . . just in time for the wedding of her two wonderful friends: Aladdin and Jamelia.

"Thank you, Kittie!" they cried.

All too soon it was
time to go home.
But what about the genie?

The genie magicked a new home in fairyland village where she could still grant wishes every now and then – especially for her friend Kittie Lacey, the best hairdresser in all the land.

Granting styling wishes since once upon a time

Kittie's Cuts

Miss Peep's Wool Shop

Mermaid's Aquatic Pets

Dr T. Fairy Crowning Glory Dentistry

Alice's Tea Room

Dr Charming's Surgery